Design : John McConnell
Article used by permission of Esquire Magazine
Excerpts from Lillian Roxon's Rock Encyclopedia used by permission

Wise Publications
London/New York/Sydney

Exclusive Distributors :
Music Sales Limited,
78 Newman Street,
London, W1P 3LA

Music Sales Australia Pty Limited
27 Clarendon Street,
Artarmon, Sydney,
Australia 2064

ROCK N' ROLL

CONTENTS

BEATLES

THE BEATLES/*Paul McCartney (piano, fuzz bass, guitar, vocals), John Lennon (harmonica, guitar, piano, vocals), George Harrison (sitar, lead guitar), Ringo Starr (Richard Starkey) (drums, organ).*
Previous members: Peter Best (drums), Stu Sutcliffe.
The day Paul McCartney was born, the number one song on the hit parade was *Sleepy Lagoon* played by Harry James. If it wasn't Harry James in those days, it was Glenn Miller, and if not Glenn Miller, Benny Goodman or Guy Lombardo or Woody Herman. Paul, John, George and Ringo were born in the forties, the era of the Big Bands. The world was at war and the songs were escapist—moonlight cocktails, sleepy lagoons and white Christmases. Bing Crosby didn't want to be fenced in, the Andrews Sisters drank rum and Coca Cola, and Perry Como was a prisoner of love when the Beatles were in their young boyhood. Later it was Peggy Lee, Nat King Cole, Dinah Shore and Frankie Laine who dominated the airwaves and the best-seller charts. Popular music was sung by adults for adults in the forties. Was there anyone else who mattered in the forties but adults? No one else was buying records, anyway, and that's what mattered.

It wasn't until the Beatles got into their teens, in the fifties that something happened that was destined to change the face of popular music and to lay the groundwork for the revolution the Beatles themselves were to bring about in the sixties. That something was Bill Haley's *Rock Around The Clock*, a song that, while it was sung by an adult, was distinctly addressed to the younger generation. It had nothing to do with cocktails and moonlight and a lot to do with being young and rebellious. The Beatles were exactly the right age to be hit hard by that song when it came out in 1955. That was the year John, fifteen and still in school, started his own group, the Quarrymen. When the historic meeting between Quarryman Lennon and new friend Paul McCartney took place on June 15, 1956, Elvis Presley's first hit, *Heartbreak Hotel*, had been number one on the U.S. hit parade for eight consecutive weeks. One of the big attractions Paul, just fourteen, had for the worldly sixteen-year-old John, was that he looked a bit like Elvis. England was absolutely Elvis-happy at the time and, of course, rock-happy. Plastic Elvises sprang up everywhere with Tommy Steele and Cliff Richard getting the same hysterical screaming adulation in England that Elvis had in the States. Paul joined the Quarrymen. He and John started writing songs together and, in 1957, when Elvis was singing *All Shook Up* and *Teddy Bear* and *Jailhouse Rock* and the Everly Brothers were singing *Wake Up Little Susie*, John and Paul wrote *Love Me Do*, which five years later in 1962 would be their first English (though not American) release.

In 1958 George Harrison, who wore tight pants and had a group called The Rebels, disbanded it to join the Quarrymen. In August of that year, when the group performed at the Casbah Club in Liverpool, the big hit was *Volare* and the latest plastic Elvis was Ricky Nelson. The Kingston Trio were about to put folk on the charts with *Tom Dooley*, beginning a folk revolution that would make Bob Dylan possible three years later in 1961. And a young man named Phil Spector in a group called the Teddy Bears had a number one record, *To Know Him Is To Love Him*. A lot of big things were starting to happen in 1958, but who could possibly know then that the Beatles were among them?

In 1959 the Quarrymen changed their name several times, ending up with the Silver Beatles. Out in the world Frankie Avalon was singing *Venus* and Elvis was still king with *Are You Lonesome Tonight?* 1960 was the year of Mark Dinning's *Teen Angel* and Ray Charles' *Georgia On My Mind*. The Silver Beatles went to Hamburg to back up a singer named Tony Sheridan. You can still buy the recordings they made there, just as a backup group. They did a sort of rock version of *My Bonnie* with Sheridan around that time. They were pretty terrible. Or, to be more generous, utterly undistinguished. People are fond of saying now that there were a hundred groups in Liverpool playing better music than the

Beatles in those days. Let's hope so. It was only in Hamburg that they started to get themselves together as a group. George, Paul, John, Peter Best on drums, Stu Sutcliffe on guitar. Their image was very rough-trade rocker, all leather and menace, as opposed to the more established rocker look of another English group in Hamburg at the time, Rory Storme and the Hurrycanes, who wore drape-shape suits with curved lapels and string ties. Their drummer, Ringo Starr, would eventually join the Beatles, but not before he learned to brush his hair forward instead of up and back in a greasy pompadour.

There were several Hamburg visits with increasingly triumphant returns to Liverpool. Then, just when kids were buying Ricky Nelson's *Travellin' Man*, in fact, the very week Dion's *Runaround Sue* was number one, someone asked Brian Epstein, a record salesman, for a record called *My Bonnie* by the Beatles. That was October 28, 1961, a big date, and if the rest isn't history, it ought to be. Epstein, made curious by this and other inquiries, tracked the group down to a place called the Cavern, where they were very popular. He became their manager and by the end of 1961 they were Liverpool's number one group—and the number one song was the Marvelettes' *Please Mr. Postman*. (Now you know why the Beatles recorded it). In 1962 everything happened. Epstein, after an eternity of pushing and wheedling and a million rejections, got the group a record contract. Ringo shaved his beard, took the grease out of his hair, put away the drape-shape suit and joined the group, replacing Peter Best. John Lennon got married. The Twist was the only thing happening on a very stale scene, but a young kid named Bob Dylan had just made a folk record and a new American group called the Beach Boys had a single out called *Surfin' Safari*. The week the Beatles' first single, *Love Me Do*, was released in England, the number one record in America was the Four Seasons' *Sherry*, which shows exactly where America was at that time. *Love Me Do* made the top twenty in England (but was not a number one record). It was released in the U.S., where everyone was listening to the *Monster Mash* and *Big Girls Don't Cry*. In the four weeks it took their next single, *Please Please Me*, to rocket its way to number one in England, America listened to *Go Away Little Girl* and *Hey Paula*. America would not hear of the Beatles for another two years.

Now it was the beginning of 1963 and the year Beatlemania happened in England. The *Please Please Me* album was number one on the charts for six months. In 1963 the group also released *From Me To You*, but it was *She Loves You* that clinched it for them and *I Want To Hold Your Hand* that set the final seal on Beatlemania. In America it was still Bobby Vinton singing *Blue Velvet*, but not for long. In a matter of weeks, at the beginning of 1964, the Beatles had displaced Vinton on the American hit parade with *I Want To Hold Your Hand*, number one for seven weeks (including the weeks the Beatles came to America, February 7 to February 21). *I Want To Hold Your Hand* was immediately followed by *She Loves You*, *Can't Buy Me Love* and *Love Me Do*, which meant that the Beatles were heading the U.S. charts from the beginning of February till the end of July, probably the biggest feat of its kind in history. When they finally were replaced, it was not by American groups but by other English groups, the Animals and Manfred Mann. The English invasion had started in earnest. The only American sound that was able to grow in influence during that British-dominated time was the Motown sound of the Supremes, which greatly influenced the Beatles and other English groups. Bob Dylan, at that time, was prophetically warning that *The Times They Are A-Changin'*, and in 1965 his prophecy came true. For the Beatles it was the end of being just another successful rock group and the beginning of serious musical maturity with *RUBBER SOUL* (in which the Beatles, for the first time, produced head music), an album very much influenced by Dylan, especially in Lennon and McCartney's lyrics. For Dylan it was another change: influenced by the Beatles—in *HIGHWAY 61 REVISITED* and *BRINGING IT ALL BACK HOME*—he went electric. As Dylan's folk went rock and the Beatles' rock went folk, 1965 was also the year of folk-rock and the Byrds (it was Byrd David Crosby who turned George Harrison on to the sitar).

The times continued to change. 1966 was the Beatles at their most Dylany with songs like the mocking *Nowhere Man*, a far cry from their early lyrics of teen love (Lennon directly, and frequently, credits Dylan for the change). And if the Beatles had changed, it was nothing to what was happening to the Beach Boys—and there were others. All of a sudden, in 1966: Simon and Garfunkel, the Mamas and the Papas, the Lovin' Spoonful, Donovan, the Stones—all coming out with something more than music had been till then. And to top it all, Dylan's *BLONDE ON BLONDE*. (Dylan, as usual, always a jump ahead.) By 1967 the Beatles were into the electronic intricacies of *SERGEANT PEPPER* (anything to top the Beach Boys' *PET SOUNDS*, *Good Vibrations* and a work in progress, *SMILE*, reportedly the greatest thing that had happened in rock to date). The Bee Gees and the Monkees dutifully stepped into the shoes the Beatles had by now outworn. Eventually *SMILE* didn't happen, Dylan was silenced by a motorcycle accident and the Beatles just about had the year to themselves, except for the emerging San Francisco scene. By 1968 Dylan was back, topping the elaborate *SERGEANT PEPPER* with an artfully simple *JOHN WESLEY HARDING*; the Beach Boys, cowed by the disaster of *SMILE*, were no longer, for the moment, a force to be reckoned with; but Cream and the Jimi Hendrix Experience and the San Francisco groups captured the popular imagination. Privately, it was a torturous time for the Beatles. Nevertheless (the Dylan influence again), they closed the year not with a new *PEPPER* but with a double album of great simplicity, a nostalgic look at rock styles.

The simplicity was misleading since, away from the studio, Beatle lives were increasingly complex. John divorced and married Japanese filmmaker Yoko Ono (with a lie-in here and a peace crusade there), Paul married American photographer Linda Eastman, George and his wife were busted, and Ringo landed in the movies. Their enthusiasm for Indian religion turned to an enthusiam for big business, with the group starting their own record company, Apple. On the Apple label, Paul presented Mary Hopkin; George presented Jackie Lomax; John presented Yoko Ono, the pair of them sweetly naked on the record's cover; Ringo stayed in the movies.

Albums/BEATLES—THIS IS WHERE IT STARTED with Tony Sheridan and the Titans: *My Bonnie; Cry For A Shadow; Saints; Why* (with Sheridan); *Johnson Rag; Darktown Strutters' Ball; Rye Beat; Summertime Beat* (the Titans); *Swanee River; You Are My Sunshine* (Sheridan & Beat Brothers). THIS IS THE SAVAGE YOUNG BEATLES with Peter Best and Tony Sheridan (Hamburg, 1961): *Cry For A Shadow; Let's Dance; If You Love Me; Baby What I Say; Why; Sweet Georgia Brown; Baby Jane; Ya-Ya*. MEET THE BEATLES (January 1964): *I Want To Hold Your Hand; I Saw Her Standing There; This Boy; It Won't Be Long; All I've Got To Do; All My Loving; Don't Bother Me; Little Child; Till There Was You; Hold Me Tight; I Wanna Be Your Man; Not A Second Time*. BEATLES' SECOND ALBUM (April 1964): *Roll Over Beethoven; Thank You Girl; Devil In Her Heart; You Really Got A Hold On Me; Money; You Can't Do That; Long Tall Sally; I Call Your Name; Please Mr. Postman; I'll Get You; She Loves You*. A HARD DAY'S NIGHT (June 1964): *A Hard Day's Night; I Should Have Known Better; If I Fell; I'm Happy Just To Dance With You; And I Love Her; Tell Me Why; Can't Buy Me Love; Any Time At All; I'll Cry Instead; Ringo's Theme (This Boy)*. SOMETHING NEW (July 1964): *I'll Cry Instead; Things We Said Today; Any Time At All; When I Get Home; Slow Down; Matchbox; Tell Me Why; And I Love Her; I'm Happy Just To Dance With You; If I Fell; Komm, Gib Mir Deine Hand*. AIN'T SHE SWEET (July 1964): *Ain't She Sweet; Sweet Georgia Brown; Nobody's Child; Take Out Some Insurance On Me Baby* (Beatles); *I Wanna Be Your Man; I Want To Hold Your Hand; She Loves You; How Do You Do It; Please Please Me; I'll Keep You Satisfied; I'm Telling You Now; From Me To You* (Swallows). BEATLES' STORY (January 1965): *On Stage With The Beatles; How Beatlemania Began; Beatlemania In Action; Man Behind The Beatles—Brian Epstein; John Lennon; Who's A Millionaire; The Beatles Look At Life; "Victims" Of Beatlemania; Beatle Medley; Ringo Starr; Liverpool And All The World!; Beatles Will Be Beatles; Man Behind The Music—George Martin; George Harrison; A Hard Day's Night; Paul McCartney; Sneaky Haircuts*. BEATLES '65 (January 1965): *No Reply; I'm A Loser; Baby's In Black;*

Rock And Roll Music; I'll Follow The Sun; She's A Woman; Mr. Moonlight; Honey Don't; I'll Be Back; I Feel Fine; Everybody's Trying To Be My Baby. EARLY BEATLES (March 1965): *Love Me Do; Twist And Shout; Anna; Chains; Ask Me Why; Boys; Please Please Me; P.S. I Love You; Baby It's You; Taste Of Honey; Do You Want To Know A Secret*. BEATLES VI (June 1965): *Kansas City; Eight Days A Week; You Like Me Too Much; Bad Boy; I Don't Want To Spoil The Party; Words Of Love; Yes It Is; Dizzy Miss Lizzy; Tell Me What You See; Every Little Thing; What You're Doing*. HELP! (August 1965): *Help; Night Before; From Me To You Fantasy; You've Got To Hide Your Love Away; I Need You; In The Tyrol; Another Girl; Another Hard Day's Night; Ticket To Ride; Bitter End; You're Gonna Lose That Girl; The Chase*. RUBBER SOUL (December 1965): *I've Just Seen A Face; Norwegian Wood; You Won't See Me; Think For Yourself; The Word; Michelle; It's Only Love; Girl; I'm Looking Through You; In My Life; Wait; Run For Your Life*. YESTERDAY AND TODAY (June 1966): *Yesterday; Drive My Car; I'm Only Sleeping; Nowhere Man; Dr. Robert; Act Naturally; And Your Bird Can Sing; If I Needed Someone; We Can Work It Out; What Goes On; Day Tripper*. REVOLVER (August 1966): *Yellow Submarine; Eleanor Rigby; Taxman; Love To You; Here, There and Everywhere; She Said She Said; Good Day Sunshine; For No One; I Want To Tell You; Got To Get You Into My Life; Tomorrow Never Knows*. SERGEANT PEPPER'S LONELY HEARTS CLUB BAND (June 1967): *Sergeant Pepper's Lonely Hearts Club Band; A Little Help From My Friends; Lucy In The Sky With Diamonds; Getting Better; Fixing A Hole; She's Leaving Home; Being For The Benefit Of Mr. Kite; Within You Without You; When I'm Sixty-Four; Lovely Rita; Good Morning Good Morning; Sergeant Pepper's Lonely Hearts Club Band—Reprise; A Day In The Life*. MAGICAL MYSTERY TOUR (November 1967): *Magical Mystery Tour; The Fool On The Hill; Flying; Blue Jay Way; Your Mother Should Know; I Am The Walrus; Hello Goodbye; Strawberry Fields Forever; Penny Lane; Baby You're A Rich Man; All You Need Is Love*. THE BEATLES (November 1968): *Back In The U.S.S.R.; Dear Prudence; Glass Onion; Ob-La-Di, Ob-La-Da; Wild Honey Pie; The Continuing Story Of Bungalow Bill; While My Guitar Gently Weeps; Happiness Is A Warm Gun; Martha My Dear; I'm So Tired; Blackbird; Piggies; Rocky Raccoon; Don't Pass Me By; Why Don't We Do It In The Road; I Will; Julia; Birthday; Yer Blues; Mother Nature's Son; Everybody's Got Something To Hide Except Me And My Monkey; Sexy Sadie; Helter Skelter; Long, Long, Long; Revolution 1; Honey Pie; Savoy Truffle; Cry Baby Cry; Revolution 9; Good Night*. YELLOW SUBMARINE (February 1969): *Yellow Submarine; Only A Northern Song; All Together Now; Hey Bulldog; It's All Too Much; All You Need Is Love; Pepperland Sea To Time & Sea Of Holes; March Of The Meanies; Sea Of Monsters; Pepperland Laid Waste; Yellow Submarine In Pepperland*.

Singles/*I Want To Hold Your Hand/I Saw Her Standing There* (January 1964); *Can't Buy Me Love/You Can't Do That* (March 1964); *A Hard Day's Night/I Should Have Known Better* (July 1964); *I'll Cry Instead/I'm Happy Just To Dance With You* (July 1964); *And I Love Her/If I Fell* (July 1964); *Slow Down/Matchbox* (August 1964); *Ain't She Sweet/Nobody's Child* (September 1964); *Sweet Georgia Brown/Take Out Some Insurance On Me Baby* (September 1964); *I Feel Fine/She's A Woman* (November 1964); *Four By The Beatles* (February 1965); *Eight Days A Week/I Don't Want To Spoil The Party* (February 1965); *Ticket To Ride/Yes It Is* (May 1965); *Help!/I'm Down* (July 1965); *Act Naturally/Yesterday* (September 1965); *We Can Work It Out/Day Tripper* (December 1965); *Nowhere Man/What Goes On* (February 1966); *Paperback Writer/Rain* (May 1966); *Yellow Submarine/Eleanor Rigby* (August 1966); *Baby, You're A Rich Man/All You Need Is Love* (October 1966); *Strawberry Fields Forever/Penny Lane* (February 1967); *Hello Goodbye/I Am The Walrus* (November 1967); *Lady Madonna/The Inner Light* (March 1968); *Hey Jude/Revolution* (July 1968); *Get Back/Don't Let Me Down* (May 1969); *Ballad of John and Yoko/Old Brown Shoe* (June 1969).

Back In The U.S.S.R.

8

Geor-gia's al-ways on my mi - mi-mi-mi-mi-mi-mi-mi mind _____ (Aw c'mon)

F7   Eb7   Bb   C7   F7

Coda   D.S. 𝄋 𝄋

Well the

Bb   Bbm   Bb

Coda

Back in the U. S. S. R. _____ Oh yeah

Bb   Eb E F

Shouts etc. ad lib.

Bb   Bb

D.S. al ⊕
D.S. al ⊕⊕

I Want To Hold Your Hand

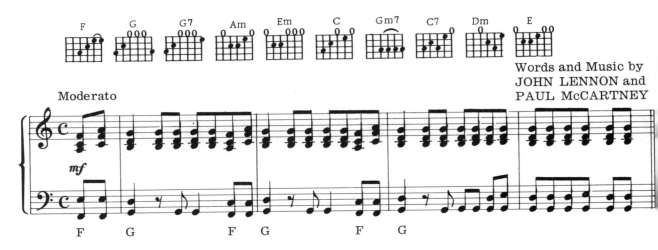

Words and Music by
JOHN LENNON and
PAUL McCARTNEY

Moderato

Oh yeh I'll _____ tell you some - thing
Please _____ say to me _____
You _____ got that some - thing

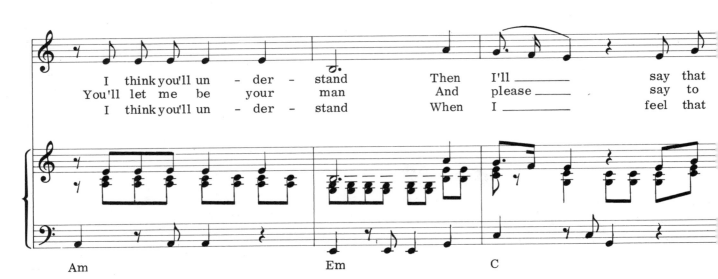

I think you'll un - der - stand   Then   I'll _____   say that
You'll let me be your man   And   please _____   say to
I think you'll un - der - stand   When   I _____   feel that

12

Lady Madonna

Words and Music by
JOHN LENNON and
PAUL McCARTNEY

14

DAVID BOWIE

DAVID BOWIE produced his first LP in 1967 and then dropped out of music completely for a while to devote his time to the Tibet Society.

Next joined a mime company, acting, writing and producing. Six months later he formed his own mime, music, mixed media trio before deciding to go solo again. States that this period of mime helps with his stage act.

The first song to gain him any public recognition was "Space Oddity", a weird, floating song of bitterness and fear. Although the single reached the charts, the album that followed, "Man Of Words Man Of Music" failed to gain him huge public acceptance.

"Oh You Pretty Things" was the first single recorded by Peter Noone on his solo career and gained David further public attention together with his taste in dress. "All The Young Dudes" recorded by Mott The Hoople and his own "John I'm Only Dancing" went into the charts in 1972. Late 1972, early 1973 sees David with four LP's in the British Top 50 and his single "The Jean Genie" reaching number 1 whilst in America his single "Space Oddity", re-released, is climbing the charts together with two LP's in the Top 100.

Married to a girl called Angie, they have one son named Zowie.

Singles
SPACE ODDITY/WILD EYED BOY FROM FREE-CLOUD (11.7.69).
CHANGES/ANDY WARHOL (7.1.72).
STARMAN/SUFFRAGETTE CITY (14.4.72).
JOHN I'M ONLY DANCING/HANG ONTO YOURSELF (1.9.72).
THE JEAN GENIE/ZIGGY STARDUST (24.11.72).

Albums
HUNKY DORY RCA SF 8244 (released December 1971).
Changes – Oh! You Pretty Things – Eight Line Poem – Life on Mars – Kooks – Quicksand – Fill Your Heart – Andy Warhol – Song For Bob Dylan – Queen Bitch – Bewlay Brothers.
THE RISE AND FALL OF ZIGGY STARDUST AND THE SPIDERS FROM MARS RCA SF 8287 (released June 1972).
Five Years – Soul Love – Moonage Daydream – Starman – It Ain't Easy – Lady Stardust – Star – Hang Onto Yourself – Ziggy Stardust – Suffragette City – Rock 'n' Roll Suicide.
MAN OF WORDS MAN OF MUSIC re-released as SPACE ODDITY RCA LSP 4813 (December 1972).
Space Oddity – Unwashed And Somewhat Slightly Dazed – Letter To Hermione – Cygnet Committee – Janine – An Occasional Dream – The Wild Eyed Boy From Freecloud – God Know's I' God – Memory Of A Free Festival.
THE MAN WHO SOLD THE WORLD RCA LSP 4816 (released December 1972).
The Width Of A Circle – All The Madmen – Black Country Rock – After All – Running Gun Blues – Saviour Machine – She Shook Me Cold – The Man Who Sold The World – The Supermen.

The Jean Genie

Words and Music by
DAVID BOWIE

CHORUS

Poor lit-tle Green-ie.__ The Jean Gen-ie

lives on his back__ The Jean Gen-ie loves chim-ney stacks__ he's out-rag-eous, he

screams and he bawls__ The Jean Gen-ie let your-self go.__

B

A

D

1 2 *D. S. al Coda* ⊕ *CODA*

A D A D

The Jean Gen-ie lives on his back___ The Jean Gen-ie loves chim-ney stacks

he's out - rag-eous, he screams and he bawls___ The Jean Gen-ie let your-self go___

B

A   D   A   D   A

D   E

John, I'm Only Dancing

Words and Music by
DAVID BOWIE

Fast rock tempo

Well, An-nie's pretty neat — she al-ways eats her meat
Ah back street love is quick and clean Life's a well thumbed machine I

Joe is aw-ful strong bet your life he's put-ting us on Oh Lord-y
saw you watching from the stairs you're ev-'ry-one who ev-er cared

Oh Lord-y You know I need some lov-ing

22

23

JOE COCKER

JOE COCKER/ A white English singer with a strong soul voice like something out of Motown, whose version of the Beatles' *With A Little Help From My Friends,* complete with female gospel chorus, caused a sensation when it was released in the U.S. in 1968. Since then he and his Grease Band have toured the United States where they have been most enthusiastically received.

Singles/*Marjorine/New Age Of The Lily; With A Little Help From My Friends/Something's Coming On* (October 1968).

Delta Lady

Words and Music by
LEON RUSSELL

Feelin' Alright

Words and Music by
DAVE MASON

1. Seems I've got to have a change of scene,
2. Well, boy you sure took me for one big ride,
3. Don't get too lost in all I say,

'cause ev - 'ry night I have the strang - est dreams;
and ev - en now I sit and won - der why,
'tho at the time I real - ly felt that way,

Im - pri - soned by the way it could have been,
That when I think of you I start to cry,
But that was then; Now it's to - day,

I left here on my own, or so it seems.
just can't waste my time, I must keep dry.
I can't get off so I'm here to stay.

CREAM

CREAM/*Eric Clapton (lead guitar), Ginger Baker (drums), Jack Bruce (bass, harmonica, vocals).*

Cream was the first of the superbluesgroups. Born of the musician's perennial dream of bringing together the cream of the current musical crop into one mind-boggling all-star group, Cream brought together Ginger Baker, master drummer, Eric Clapton, king of the English blues guitarists, and Jack Bruce, superbass. This was early 1967, when those who had outgrown early Beatles and early Beatles imitators were ready to get their teeth into some adult and substantial music, so their timing was perfect.

With Cream rock finally grew up, and Eric Clapton became the all-time rock hero, edging Lennon and Jagger from their pedestals. Although there's been plenty of blues playing around, it took Cream to fully tune a whole new generation in to that kind of music. Cream was almost entirely responsible for the blues revival of 1968 and for the great interest in the roots of the new blues-rock. Clapton and Mike Bloomfield (of the Paul Butterfield Blues Band and the Electric Flag) continually gave credit where it was due, talking of roots and sources, bringing up the names of blues originals like B. B. King, Muddy Waters and Howlin' Wolf. It worked two ways for them, for once some of the more astute heard the originals they were less impressed by what Cream and the Bloomfield bands were doing. But that was irrelevant because Cream conquered like no other band did, so that by the end of 1968, when they called it quits, they were able to sell out New York's enormous Madison Square Garden weeks before their "farewell" concert.

To hear them was to be left stoned and stunned. No one had quite seen anything like the way Cream worked—not as an uninspired background for a brilliant soloist, but three major musicians giving it everything from start to finish. In spite of Clapton, there were no stars, just the music. There had been several seasons of delicate imagery, Donovan and the other poets; Cream gave it out hot and heavy and very physical, which is not to say there was no delicate imagery. Martin Sharp's lyrics for *Tales Of Brave Ulysses* are among the most beautiful in the new rock. Clapton's guitar (you knew he had listened and played with every blues record ever made, all the way back to the Mississippi Delta) was as lean and melancholy as his face. Jack Bruce—who could believe he had played on Manfred Mann's hit *Pretty Flamingo*—was the embodiment of music: instrumentalist, vocalist and composer. Ginger Baker was the devil with drumsticks. Each gave the others a run for their money, frantically competing for attention, though never at the cost of what they were playing. In any case, all of them were always winning, which was what made the music so heavy and rich.

Cream's music was essentially interpretative blues and rock, with all kinds of personal versatility but very little cheap flash, and no help from musical friends, except on their last album, in which they did use sidemen. The group always came off better live than on album, and when *WHEELS OF FIRE* was made, as a two-record set, one record was live. There were criticisms of the albums (after all, the standards set by Cream were high) and there were personal problems (Clapton, particularly, seemed unable to cope with the lack of time and thinking space), but all the same, it came as a great shock, just when they could be said to be the number one group in America, to hear their announcement that they would disband. The only possible consolation at that time was the thought that out of the break could come, after some cunning

contractual reshuffling in other circles, not one supergroup like Cream, but three, with Bruce, Baker and Clapton each heading one.

And where was Cream when all the other English groups were happening, from 1964 on? Bruce, who started off singing Scots folk songs, was in the Graham Bond Organization, an organ group with jazz and blues influences with which jazz-oriented Ginger Baker also played. Bruce also played with the highly commercial Manfred Mann group for a while, and with the blues-oriented John Mayall Blues Breakers, the group Eric Clapton went to after starting with the Yardbirds. You can hear echoes of all these groups in a Cream performance, for they all had a lot to teach a young musician, but the format had always been too rigid. Cream represented unheard-of freedom for the three, at first anyway. Now that the band is finished, its legacy is everywhere. Until Cream, few groups thought of having solos; now even Ginger Baker's drum solo *Toad* is widely imitated. Other groups, seeing Cream's huge success with albums rather than "commercial" singles, finally dared to move out of pop back into music—and record companies approved. There is a lot to thank Cream for: the new enthusiasm for blues, the new enthusiasm for rock generally.

Albums/FRESH CREAM (January 1967): *I Feel Free; N.S.U.; Sleepy Time Time; I'm So Glad; Toad; Dreaming; Sweet Wine; Cat's Squirrel; Four Until Late; Rollin' And Tumblin'.* DISRAELI GEARS (December 1967): *Strange Brew; Sunshine Of Your Love; Blue Condition; World Of Pain; Dance The Night Away; Tales Of Brave Ulysses; Swlabr; We're Going Wrong; Outside Woman Blues; Take It Back; Mother's Lament.* WHEELS OF FIRE (June 1968): *White Room; Sitting On Top Of The World; Passing The Time; As You Said; Pressed Rat And Warthog; Politician; Those Were The Days; Born Under A Bad Sign; Deserted Cities Of The Heart; Crossroads; Spoonful; Traintime; Toad. Goodbye; I'm So Glad; Politician; Sitting On Top Of The World; What A Bringdown; Doing That Scrapyard Thing; Badge.* GOODBYE: *Sitting on top of the World; Badge; Doing that Scrapyard Thing; What a Bringdown; I'm so Glad; Politician.*

Singles/*I Feel Free/N.S.U.* (January 1967); *Strange Brew/ Tales Of Brave Ulysses* (May 1967); *Spoonful* (2 Parts) (September 1967); *Swlabr/Sunshine Of Your Love* (December 1967); *Pressed Rat And Warthog/Anyone For Tennis* (March 1968); *White Room/Those Were The Days* (September 1968).

Also Appear On/SAVAGE SEVEN: *Anyone For Tennis; Desert Ride.*

Strange Brew

Words and Music by
ERIC CLAPTON and
FELIX PAPPALARDI

Strange brew kill-ing what's in-side of you. She's a

witch of trou-ble in e-lec-tric blue. In her own mad mind she's in
some kind of dem-on dust-ing in the flue. If you don't watch out then she'll

36

Sunshine Of Your Love

Words and Music by
JACK BRUCE, PETE BROWN
and ERIC CLAPTON

38

CREEDANCE CLEARWATER REVIVAL

CREEDENCE CLEARWATER REVIVAL/*Doug Clifford (drums), Stuart Cook (electric bass, piano), John Fogerty (guitar, harp, piano, organ), Tom Fogerty (guitar).*
Rock and roll wasn't dead in 1968. It was just playing possum. Creedence Clearwater Revival proved that by reviving a mid-fifties hit *Suzie Q* and making it a mid-sixties hit, though they were an unknown group. Since then the group has established itself comfortably as one of the big groups of 1969.

Albums/CREEDENCE CLEARWATER REVIVAL: *Ninety-nine And A Half; I Put A Spell On You; Working Man; Walk On The Water; Gloomy; Get Down Woman; Suzie Q; Porterville.* BAYOU COUNTRY: *Born On The Bayou; Bootleg; Graveyard Train; Penthouse Pauper; Proud Mary; Keep On Chooglin'.*

Singles/*Suzie Q/I Put A Spell On You; Proud Mary/Born On The Bayou; Lodi/Bad Moon Rising* (May 1969).

Bad Moon Rising

Words and Music by
JOHN C. FOGERTY

Proud Mary

Words and Music by
JOHN C. FOGERTY

Moderately *(with a heavy beat)*

VERSE G

Left a good job___ in the ci - ty,___ Work - in' for The Man ev'ry night and day,___
Cleaned a lot of plates in Mem - phis, Pumped a lot of pain down in New Or - leans,___

And I nev - er lost one min - ute of sleep - in', Wor - ry - in' 'bout the way things might have been.___
But I nev - er saw the good side of the ci - ty, Un - til I hitched a ride on a riv - er boat queen.___

CHORUS

D

Big wheel___ keep on ___ turn - in',___

Em

Proud Mar - y keep on bur'n - in',___ Roll-

Up Around The Bend

Words and Music by
JOHN C. FOGERTY

VERSE

1. There's a place___ up a-head___ and I'm go-in' Just as fast___ as my feet___ can fly___

Come a-way,___ come a-way___ if you're go-in',

CHORUS

Leave the sink-in' ship___ be-hind. Come on the ris-in' wind,___

FREE

FREE paid their dues in the dawning era of rock music, taking their uniquely individual music around the clubs and back-room concert halls of the late-sixties' English blues scene and helping to drag a newly-discovered musical discipline from naive adolescence to proud maturity.

It was late in 1968 with a growing and loyal following behind them and a Marquee residency (then a rare and privileged status symbol) to their credit, that Free first went into the studio and recorded their first album, "Tons Of Sobs", confirming their reputation as one of the brightest hopes on a then-barren musical scene.

By October 1969, when they released their second album, "Free", the band had built up a reputation and following. When the band released their third album, "Fire And Water" in 1970, it went to the top of the album charts throughout Britain, America and the Continent and "All Right Now" taken from it turned Free into Stars.

Paul Rodgers – Vocals, Guitar
Simon Kirke – Drums
Rabbit – Keyboards
Tetsu – Bass

Alright Now

**Words and Music by
PAUL FRASER and
ANDY FRASER**

Fire And Water

Words and Music by
ANDY FRASER and
PAUL RODGERS

56

Little Bit Of Love

Words and Music by
PAUL RODGERS,
ANDY FRASER,
PAUL KOSSOF
and SIMON KIRKE

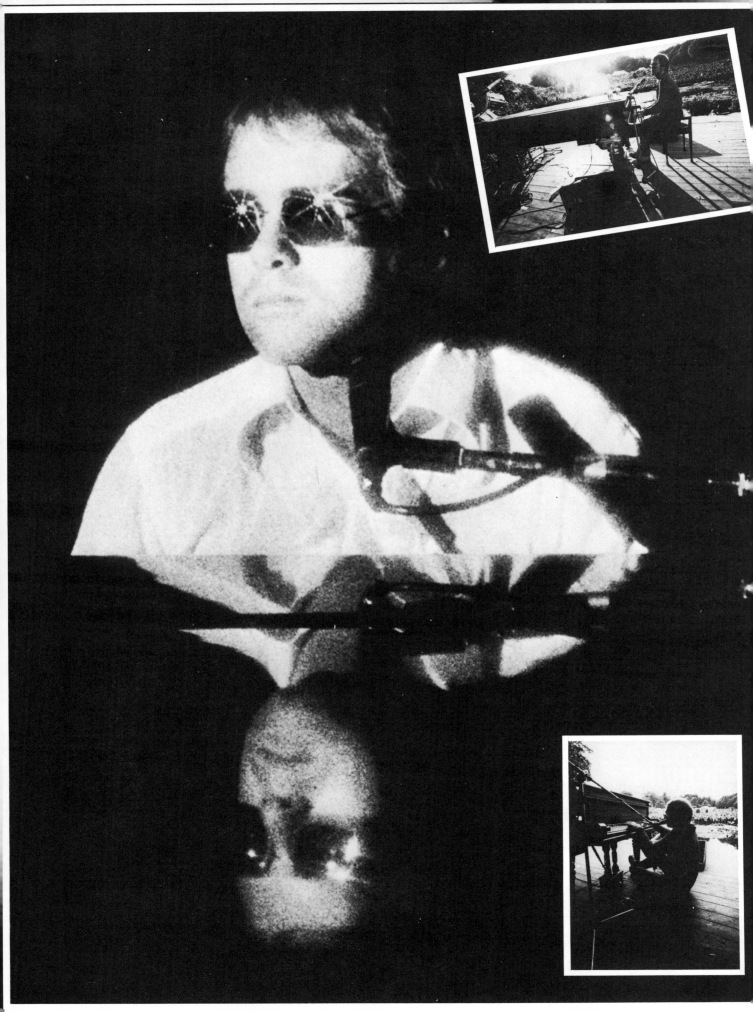

ELTON JOHN

CAT DJS 269 (August, 1972). ooCROCODILE ROCK DJS 271 (October, 1972), DANIEL DJS 275 (January, 1973).

*denotes gold album in U.S.A.
+denotes platinum album in U.S.A.
=denotes gold album in U.K.
odenotes one million sales worldwide.
odenotes quarter of million sales in U.K.

ELTON JOHN was born in Middlesex, London on March 25, 1947, and after the usual course of piano lessons, studied at the Royal Academy of Music before embarking on a pop career playing piano and organ with Bluesology and Long John Baldry. Elton soon began to write his own material, teaming up with lyricist Bernie Taupin in response to a newspaper advertisement.

Early compositions like "Lady Samantha", "Skyline Pigeon" and his first album "Empty Sky" received acclaim from critics and musicians but there was little reaction from the general public until his second album "Elton John". This album was well received by both critics and public and he became much in demand for radio and TV appearances. His appearances in the States were wildly successful and with the arrival of his third album "Tumbleweed Connection" it became obvious that an important new force had appeared on the music scene.

Elton recorded and composed, with lyricist Bernie Taupin, the vocal compositions on the Paramount soundtrack album "Friends" for the film of the same name. A further album titled "17.11.70", taken from a live recording during Elton's second American tour in November 1970, is currently available.

There is little that needs to be said about Elton John's recent career. His appearances throughout the world are eagerly awaited and constantly acclaimed. The albums "Elton John", "Tumbleweed Connection", "Freinds", "17.11.70", "Madman Across The Water" and "Honky Chateau" have all earned gold discs and Elton's last single "Crocodile Rock" has already been awarded a silver disc in the U.K. and is rapidly moving up the American charts. Elton's career was recently crowned by his appearance at the Royal Command Performance and his new single "Daniel" and the album "Don't Shoot Me I'm Only The Piano Player" can only continue Elton's success.

His stage act with Nigel Olsson on drums, Dee Murray on bass and Davey Johnstone on guitar, combines excitement with good music and confirms his position as a leading force in pop music in the seventies.

Albums

EMPTY SKY Produced by Steve Brown DJLPS 403 (June, 1969). =+*ELTON JOHN Produced by Gus Dudgeon DJLPS 406 (April, 1970). =*TUMBLEWEED CONNECTION Produced by Gus Dudgeon DJLPS 410 (October, 1970). *17.11.70 DJLPS 414 (April, 1971). *FRIENDS (Paramount film soundtrack) (April, 1971). *MADMAN ACROSS THE WATER Produced by Gus Dudgeon DJLPH 420 (October, 1971). *HONKY CHATEAU Produced by Gus Dudgeon DJLPH 423 (May, 1972). DON'T SHOOT ME I'M ONLY THE PIANO PLAYER Produced by Gus Dudgeon DJLPH 427 (January, 1973).

Singles

LADY SAMANTHA BF 1739 (January, 1969). IT'S ME THAT YOU NEED DJS 205 (May, 1969). BORDER SONG DJS 217 (March, 1970). ROCK AND ROLL MADONNA DJS 222 (June, 1970). YOUR SONG DJS 237 (January, 1971). FRIENDS DJS 244 (April, 1971). oROCKET MAN DJX 501 (April, 1972). HONKY

Crocodile Rock

Words and Music by
ELTON JOHN and
BERNIE TAUPIN

64

Lawd-y ma - ma those Fri - day nights____ when Su - sie wore____ her

dres-ses tight_____ and the Croc-o- dile____ Rock-in' was _____ out of

sight. _____

C

1
But the years

2
I re-mem-

3

G

Em

Repeat till fa...

C

D

Honky Cat

Words and Music by
ELTON JOHN and
BERNIE TAUPIN

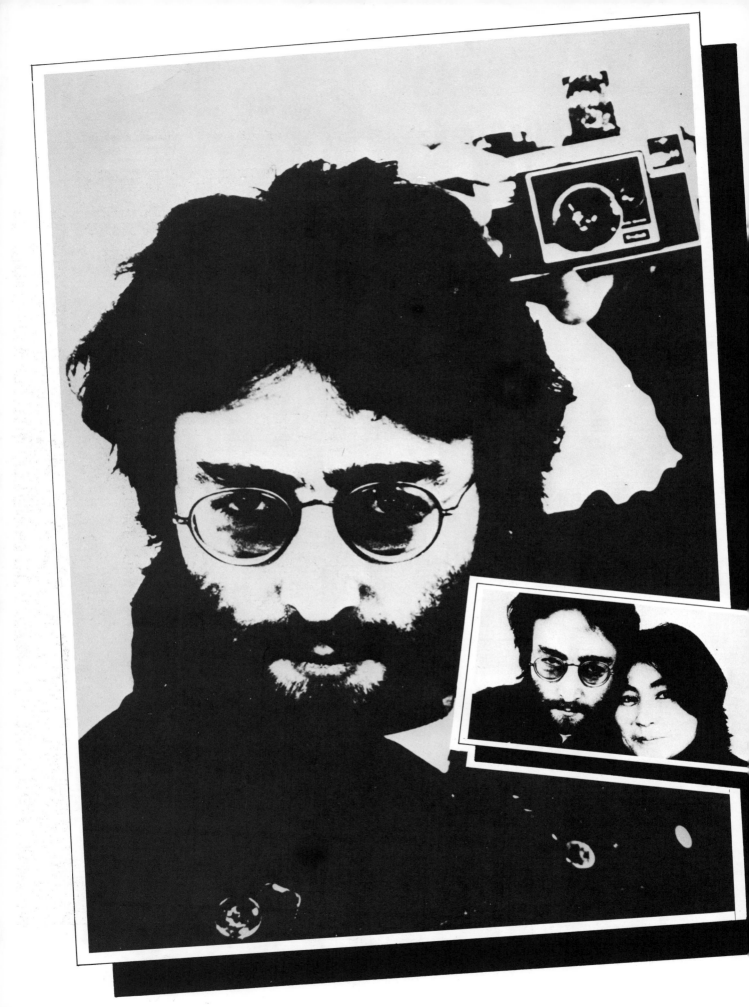

JOHN LENNON

JOHN LENNON Born: October 9, 1940 at Liverpool Maternity Hospital. Brought up by an aunt after his parents separated when he was a baby. Educated at Dovedale Primary School, Quarrybank Grammar School and Liverpool College of Art. Married Cynthia Powell on August 23, 1962 and has one son, Julian. Divorced on November 8, 1968, he married Yoko Ono on March 20, 1969 in Gibraltar. Always considered to be the leader of the Beatles, it was John who eventually decided to leave them first. Now fervently involved in extreme left wing politics, and avant garde film-making. A hero figure of the underground's establishment. Lives in New York and Ascot.

Singles
GIVE PEACE A CHANCE/REMEMBER LOVE Plastic Ono Band (4.7.69).
COLD TURKEY/DON'T WORRY KYOKO MUMMY'S ONLY LOOKING FOR HER HAND IN THE SNOW Plastic Ono Band (24.10.69).
INSTANT KARMA/WHO HAS SEEN THE WIND Plastic Ono Band (6.2.70).
POWER TO THE PEOPLE/OPEN YOUR BOX John Lennon And Yoko Ono (5.3.71).
HAPPY XMAS (WAR IS OVER)/LISTEN, THE SNOW IS FALLING John Lennon, Yoko Ono & The Plastic Ono Band (24.11.72).

Albums
TWO VIRGINS SAPCOR 2 John Lennon And Yoko Ono (29.11.68).
Two Virgins 1 – Together – Two Virgins 2 – Two Virgins 3 – Two Virgins 4 – Two Virgins 5 – Hush A Bye Hush A Bye – Two Virgins 6 – Two Virgins 7 – Two Virgins 8 – Two Virgins 9 – Two Virgins 10.
UNFINISHED MUSIC NO 2 – LIFE WITH THE LIONS ZAPPLE 01 John Lennon And Yoko Ono (2.5.69).
Cambridge 1969 – No Bed For Beatle John – Baby's Heart Beat – Two Minutes Silence – Radio Play.
WEDDING ALBUM SPACOR 11 John Lennon And Yoko Ono (14.11.69).
John And Yoko – Amsterdam.
LIVE PEACE IN TORONTO 1969 CORE 2001 The Plastic Ono Band (11.12.69).
Blue Suede Shoes – Money – Dizzy Miss Lizzie – Yer Blues – Cold Turkey – Give Peace A Chance – Don't Worry Kyoko Mummy's Only Looking For Her Hand In The Snow – John John (Let's Hope For Peace).
JOHN LENNON/PLASTIC ONO BAND PCS 7124 John Lennon & The Plastic Ono Band (11.12.70).
Mother – Hold On – I Find Out – Working Class Hero – Isolation – Remember – Love – Well Well Well – Look At Me – God – My Mummy's Dea.
IMAGINE PAS 1004 John Lennon (October 71).
Imagine – Crippled Inside – Jealous Guy – It's So Hard – I Don't Want To Be A Soldier – Gimme Some Truth – Oh My Love – How Do You Sleep – How – Oh Yoko.
SOMETIME IN NEW YORK PCSP John Lennon (15.9.72).
Woman Is The Nigger Of The World – Sisters O Sisters – Attica State – Born In A Prison – New York City

Gimme Some Truth

Words and Music by
JOHN LENNON

16 bars per minute

1.4. I'm sick and tired of hear-ing things from up-tight short sight-ed nar-row minded hyp-ocritics
2. Ad lib guitar solo -
3. I'm sick to death of see-ing things from tight-lipped condescending mommies' little chauvinists

all I want is the truth ___ Just gim-me some truth ___
all I want is the truth ___ Just gim-me some truth ___ now

I've had e-nough of read-ing things_ by neu-rot-ic psy-chot-ic pig head-ed pol-i-ti-cians
I've had e-nough of watch-ing scenes_ of schizophrenic e-go-cent-ric par-a-no-ic pri-ma don-nas

all I want is the truth ___ Just gim-me some truth _ (now) No
all I want is the truth _ now Just gim-me some truth ___

73

The Ballad Of John And Yoko

Words and Music by
JOHN LENNON

48 bars per minute

Stand-ing in the dock at South-am(p)
Final-y made the plane in-to Pa-
Pa -ris to the Am -ster-dam Hil-
Made a light -ning trip to Vi- en-
Caught the ear - ly plane back to Lon-

___ ton, ___ trying to get to Hol - land or France. ___ The
___ ris, ___ hon - ey - moon-ing down by the Seine. ___ Pe - te(r)
___ ton, ___ talk - ing in our beds for a week. ___ The
___ na, ___ eat - ting choc'-late cake in a bag. ___ The
___ don, ___ fif - ty a - corns tied in a sack. ___ The

man in the mac ___ said ___ you've got to go back ___ you know they did - n't ev - en give us a chan(ce)
Brown called to say, ___ you ___ can make it O. K., you can get mar-ried in Gib-ral - ter near Spa(in)
news-pa-pers said, ___ say what're you do-ing in bed, ___ I said we're on - ly trying to get us some pe(ace)
news-pa-pers said, ___ she's gone to his head, ___ they look just like two Gu - rus in dra(g)
men from the press ___ said ___ we wish you suc-cess, ___ it's good to have the both of you bac(k)

ROLLING STONES

ROLLING STONES/*Mick Jagger (lead vocals, harmonica), Keith Richard (lead guitar, vocals), Brian Jones (rhythm guitar, harmonica, sitar), Charlie Watts (drums), Bill Wyman (bass guitar).*

When the Beatles were still four sweet little moptop dolls in 1964, and we didn't know then that they were going to grow into more than faces on a Woolworth's charm bracelet, the Stones did not come on, as almost everyone else on the English scene did, as moptop imitations. Even at that early, early stage they did their own thing. And their thing was the full slummy English lout barrow-boy gutter-rat routine. Mean, moody and magnificent (as was once said about Jane Russell).

While the 1964 Beatles looked as if they had been personally scrubbed down by Brian Epstein himself, the 1964 Rolling Stones looked as if they had been sent to bed every night for a week with the same clothes on and no supper. By the time they hit Beatle-sated, Hermit-sated America, they looked different, not to say positively menacing. This immediately established them as personalities at a time when so many hairy groups had come through that they had all eventually become faceless. Their music had much the same impact. The Beatles' songs had been rinsed and hung out to dry. The Stones had never seen soap and water. And where the adorable little windup Beatle moptops wanted no more than to hold a hand, the hateful rasping Stones were bent on rape, pillage and plunder. Well, at least satisfaction. At that stage, both the Beatles and the Stones were doing English imitations of American music (there certainly wasn't any English music worth imitating then), but the Stones were basing their music on an earlier, earthier and less polished period than the period the Beatles were concentrating on.

English groups were into raunchy American blues before the Stones (there was a long tradition of that), but they had always done it in a very removed way—a little too earnest, a little too intent and reverent. Not Jagger. No one had ever seen a white man move on stage the way Jagger moved. Later, like Elvis, whom he completely overshadowed, he was to become the prototype for stage sexuality, the most imitated singer in rock. Right from the start he parodied himself completely, but that worked *for* him, not against him. His lips and no-hips drove every relevant point home; a not-so-distant relative of the Shangri-las' Leader of the Pack, he laid it all on the line.

Most of the girls who watched had never before had the word put on them quite so explicitly. It was heady stuff for fourteen-year-old virgins, and others besides. And the publicity played it up, although it is hard to say where manager Andrew Oldham's shrewdness left off and the Stones' own natural boorishness began. In any case, they were never photographed to look pretty; they seemed under orders not to smile and their music was full of disdain for women, morals, parents and under-assistant West Coast promotion men.

What started off as a series of straight pinches from a variety of black blues musicians of the past eventually came out as the Stones sound. Even in the first three albums, where they were simply searching for a musical identity in their vast repertoire of soul music, rhythm and blues, and Chicago blues, they were producing what was then the heaviest music to come out of England in that 1964-early 1965 period. They started to find themselves in mid-1965 in their fourth album, *OUT OF OUR HEADS* (stopping only to pay tribute to some heroes, Sam Cooke and Otis Redding), continuing the process

with *DECEMBER'S CHILDREN*, where it was clear from the growing number of Mick Jagger-Keith Richard compositions that a Stones "personality" was emerging in unambiguous lyrics and music. *BIG HITS (HIGH TIDE AND GREEN GRASS)* in the spring of 1966 was the wrap-up of that time, their sort of farewell to the first golden era.

AFTERMATH, that summer, saw something quite new. The Stones had made every point they needed to make. Now they could relax. Some of the brute force was gone now, to be replaced by tenderness, impatience and more than a touch of the sardonic. Guitarist Brian Jones played dulcimer and, in *Paint It Black,* sitar, which had hardly been used then in rock except by the Beatles and Byrds. There was early fuzztone in *Think* and a most un-Stones-like Elizabethan mood prevailed, just mocking enough to make it believable. A live album followed and *BETWEEN THE BUTTONS,* where the Stones told it all (*Let's Spend The Night Together* and *Something Happened To Me Yesterday*), then *FLOWERS* in the summer of 1967, a farewell to the second golden era.

The second golden era was marked by the highly publicized 1967 bust, the first *big* drug bust in English rock. They didn't have the sort of public image that a bust would hurt and the uncharitable never stopped insisting that manager Oldham had engineered it all, but the bust *was* a jolt to them, and two further busts of Brian Jones, harrowing, to say the least. Out of all this private confusion emerged the Stones' answer to the Beatles' *SERGEANT PEPPER* album—*THEIR SATANIC MAJESTIES REQUEST,* an album that induced more visions than anything coming out of San Francisco in the height of the psychedelic revolution. The album was not entirely a critical success and the two hard-rock singles that followed suggested a possible return to their earlier styles.

Their new album, *BEGGAR'S BANQUET,* bears this out. It is a comeback, a great rock and roll album with no pretenses, Dylanesque lyrics, and a country and western mood. For the big people in rock, 1968 was the year for a return to simplicity, and that seems to be what happened with the Rolling Stones. For a while, all seemed well. Then in June 1969, a shock: Brian Jones left to do his own music. His replacement was Mick Taylor, formerly of John Mayall's Blues Breakers. A few weeks later Brian was found dead in his swimming pool.

The group is still strong and together. Jagger is becoming a film star (*Performance* and *Ned Kelly*). But nothing is the same. How could it be?

Albums/THE ROLLING STONES (May 1964): *Not Fade Away; Route 66; I Just Want To Make Love To You; Honest I Do, Now I've Got A Witness; Little By Little; I'm King Bee; Carol; Tell Me; Can I Get A Witness; You Can Make It If You Try; Walking The Dog.* 12 X 5 (October 1964): *Around And Around; Confessin' The Blues; 2120 So. Michigan Avenue; Empty Heart; Time Is On My Side; Good Times, Bad Times; It's All Over Now; Under The Boardwalk; Grown Up Wrong; Congratulations; If You Need Me; Susie Q.* THE ROLLING STONES NOW (February 1965): *Heart Of Stone; Everybody Needs Somebody To Love; Little Red Rooster; Oh Baby We Got A Good Thing Goin'; Down Home Girl; You Can't Catch Me; What A Shame; Down The Road A Piece; Off The Hook; Pain In My Heart; Surprise, Surprise; Mona (I Need You Baby).* OUT OF OUR HEADS (July 1965): *Mercy Mercy; Hitch Hike; Last Time; That's How Strong My Love Is; Good Times; I'm All Right; Satisfaction (I Can't Get No); Cry To Me; Under Assistant West Coast Promotion Man; Play With Fire; Spider And The Fly; One More Try.* DECEMBER'S CHILDREN (November 1965): *Get Off My Cloud; Blue Turns To Grey; She Said Yeah; Talkin' About You; You Better Move On; Look What You've Done; The Singer Not The Song; Route 66; I'm Free; As Tears Go By; Gotta Get Away; I'm Moving On.* BIG HITS (HIGH TIDE AND GREEN GRASS) (March 1966): *19th Nervous Breakdown; Satisfaction (I Can't Get No); Last Time; As Tears Go By; Time Is On My Side; It's All Over Now; Tell Me; Heart Of Stone. Get Off My Cloud; Not Fade Away; Good Times, Bad Times; Play With Fire.* AFTERMATH (June 1966): *Paint It Black; Stupid Girl; Lady Jane; Think; Under My Thumb; Doncha Bother Me; Flight; High And Dry; It's Not Easy; I Am Waiting; Going.* GOT "LIVE" IF YOU WANT IT (November 1966): *Have You Seen Your*

Mother, Baby, Standing In The Shadow; Under My Thumb;
Get Off My Cloud; Lady Jane; I've been Loving You Too
Long; Fortune Teller; Last Time; 19th Nervous Breakdown;
Time Is On My Side; I'm Alright; Satisfaction (I Can't Get
No); Not Fade Away. BETWEEN THE BUTTONS (Janu-
ary 1967): *Ruby Tuesday; Let's Spend The Night Together;*
Yesterday's Papers; Connection; All Sold Out; She Smiled
Sweetly; Cool And Collected; My Obsession; Who's Been
Sleeping Here; Complicated; Miss Amanda Jones; Something
Happened To Me Yesterday. FLOWERS (June 1967): *Ruby*
Tuesday; Have You Seen Your Mother, Baby; Let's Spend

Jumpin' Jack Flash

Words and Music by
MICK JAGGER and
KEITH RICHARDS

I was born in a cross fire hur - ri - cane,
I was raised by a tooth-less bear - ded hag.
I was drowned. I was washed up and left for dead.

And I howled at my ma in the dri - ving rain.
I was schooled with a strap right across my back.
I fell down to my feet and I saw they bled,

To Coda

But it's al —— right —— now. In fact it's a gas

Honky Tonk Woman

Words and Music by
MICK JAGGER and
KEITH RICHARDS

Street Fighting Man

Words and Music by
MICK JAGGER and
KEITH RICHARDS

Ev - 'ry-where I hear the sound of march-ing, charg-ing feet, Oh, Boy. 'Cause

sum-mer's here and the time is right for fight - ing in the street, Oh, Boy. But

what can a poor boy do ex - cept to sing for a Rock'N'Roll Band 'cause in sleep-y Lon - do

Town, There's just no place for Street Fight-ing Man! _____ No!

Hey! Think the time is right for a Pal-ace Rev-o-lu-tion. ___ But

where I live the game to play is Com-pro-mise So-lu-tion! ___ Well, Then

Brown Sugar

Words and Music by
MICK JAGGER and
KEITH RICHARDS

Moderate tempo (32 bars per minute)

cot - ton fields, ____ sold ____ in a mar-ket down in New Or - leans. ____ Scarred
blood runs hot, ____ la - dy of the house won-d'rin where it's gon-na stop. House
Tent Show queen, ____ and ____ all her girl friends were sweet six - teen. ____ I'm

Gold ____ Coast slave ship bound for
Beat - ing, ____ cold Eng-lish
I bet your ma - ma was a

TRAFFIC

Alright; Vagabond Virgin, 40,000 Headmen; Cryin' To Be Heard; No Time To Live; Means To An End.
Singles/Here We Go 'Round The Mulberry Bush/Mr. Fantasy, (April 1968): Paper Sun/Coloured Rain; Smiling Phases/Hole In My Shoe; Feelin' Alright/Withering Tree (October 1968).

TRAFFIC/Stevie Winwood (piano, organ, auto-organ), Chris Wood (flute, tenor, alto and soprano sax) Jim Capaldi (drums, piano) Dave Mason (bass guitar, sitar).

Someone once asked Jerry Wexler, who produces Aretha and is therefore in a position to know something about soul, what he had to say about white soul and he said two words: Stevie Winwood. The voice, guitar, organ and piano of Traffic, Stevie is white, frail, English and one of the Renaissance men of rock—writer, arranger, performer.

The Traffic story starts with the Spencer Davis story. Davis started a group in 1963 with three others, two of whom were brothers already playing together. One of those brothers was Stevie, aged fifteen. Like the Beatles, he came out of the skiffle craze of 1959 (though he was only eleven when he was in a skiffle band). He had lived and breathed American blues from the start, learned from the record collections of friends. It was Stevie's voice, his songs, his organ and piano work that made Spencer Davis's band. I'm A Man and Gimme Some Loving, two of Stevie's songs done under the Davis umbrella, were so black and strong it took a lot of adjusting to get used to the fact that they were coming from a seventeen-year-old English kid from Birmingham. In 1967 Stevie decided to leave Davis (life on the road was bringing him down) and start his own group.

With maturity and wisdom you don't find even in older musicians, Stevie took himself and his new musicians off to a quiet country cottage in Berkshire to work and get themselves together as people, as a band, as musicians. Photographers were barred. Reporters were barred. Under assistant promotion men were barred. It was all peace and quiet there, with green grass, and roaring logs on the fire at night. An idyllic setting that was immediately reflected in the first Traffic singles, Paper Sun and Hole in My Shoe and in everything else that followed. You could see it in the way Stevie smiled, a smile with no tensions, or with the way his group moved physically on stage. They worked together so perfectly with so much telepathy and trust that sometimes the audience felt a little left out.

For a long time Traffic looked like it would be a great band, a nicely balanced blend of three or four good musicians (depending on whether Dave Mason was in or out that week). Winwood's voice was strong; Capaldi's drums were strong; Chris Wood on flute, Mason on sitar and Winwood on organ were gentle and peaceful. Traffic was in the process of changing the whole mood of popular music when Mason left, leaving a trio that worked well only when it was the then unusual organ-drums-flute combination. In the traditional guitar, bass, drums grouping it was invariably too thin. When Mason returned, all seemed to be saved and the group never seemed happier. They started to get away from the blues that had put them on the map with Spencer Davis. But Traffic wasn't to last and at the height of their popularity, to everyone's surprise, the group split, Winwood to join Clapton and Baker in Blind Faith, the other three to try and work out a combination of their own.

Albums/MR. FANTASY (March 1968): Dear Mr. Fantasy; Paper Sun; Hole In My Shoe; Dealer; Coloured Rain; No Face, No Name And No Number; Heaven Is In Your Mind; House For Everyone; Berkshire Poppies; Giving To You; Smiling Phases; We're A Fade, You Missed This. TRAFFIC (October 1968): You Can All Join In; Pearly Queen; Don't Be Sad; Who Knows What Tomorrow Will Bring; Feeling

(Roamin' Thru The Gloamin' With)
Forty Thousand Headmen

Words and Music by
STEVE WINWOOD and
JIM CAPALDI

1. For-ty thou - sand head-men could-n't make me change my mind   If I had to take the choice be-tween the
2. Had-n't tra-velled ve-ry far when sud-den-ly I saw   Three small ships a-sail-ing on-to-
4. Lay-ing down my trea-sure be -   fore the I - ron gate   Quick-ly rang the bell hop-ing — I

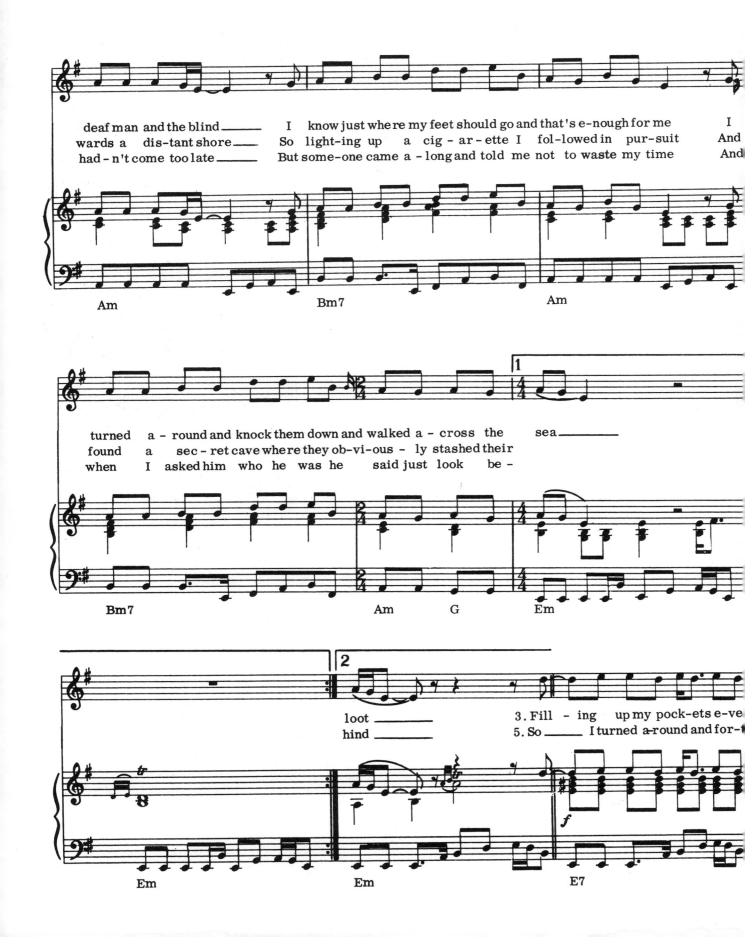

Chord Encyclopedia

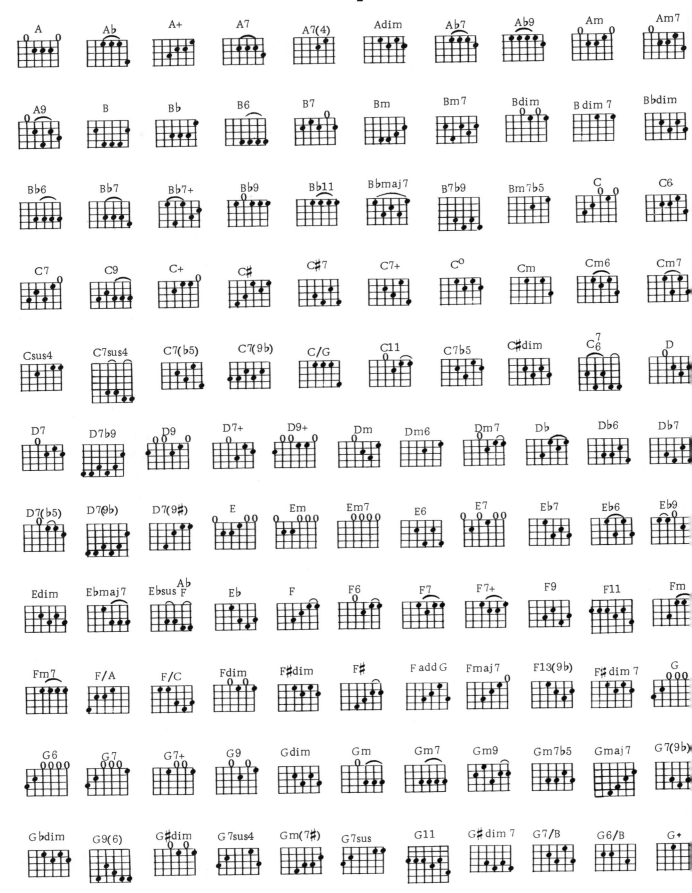